My dear mouse fr...

Have I ever told you how much ...
fiction? I've always wanted to ... in credible
adventures set in another dimension, but I've never
believed that parallel universes exist . . . until now!

That's because my good friend Professor Paws
von Volt, the brilliant, secretive scientist, has
just made an incredible discovery. Thanks to some
mousetropic calculations, he determined that there
are many different dimensions in time and space,
where anything could be possible.

The professor's work inspired me to write this
science fiction adventure in which my
family and I travel through space
in search of new worlds.
We're a fabumouse crew:
the spacemice!

I hope you enjoy this
intergalactic adventure!

Geronimo Stilton

**PROFESSOR
PAWS VON VOLT**

THE SPACEMICE

GERONIMO STILTONIX

TRAP STILTONIX

THEA STILTONIX

GRANDFATHER WILLIAM STILTONIX

ROBOTIX

BENJAMIN STILTONIX AND BUGSY WUGSY

Geronimo Stilton

SPACEMICE

ALIEN ESCAPE

Scholastic Inc.

ISBN 978-0-545-64650-5

Based on an original idea by Elisabetta Dami.

www.geronimostilton.com

Published by Scholastic Inc., 557 Broadway, New York, NY 10012. SCHOLASTIC and associated logos are trademarks and/or registered trademarks of Scholastic Inc.

Stilton is the name of a famous English cheese. It is a registered trademark of the Stilton Cheese Makers' Association. For more information, go to www.stiltoncheese.com.

Text by Geronimo Stilton
Original title *Minaccia dal pianeta Blurgo*
Cover by Flavio Ferron
Illustrations by Giuseppe Facciotto (design) and Daniele Verzini (color)
Graphics by Chiara Cebraro

Special thanks to AnnMarie Anderson
Translated by Emily Clement
Interior design by Joseph Semien

12   19/0

Printed in the U.S.A.   40
First printing, May 2014

In the darkness of the farthest galaxy in time and space is a spaceship inhabited exclusively by mice.

This fabumouse vessel is called the **MouseStar 1**, and I am its captain!

I am Geronimo Stiltonix, a somewhat accident-prone mouse who (to tell you the truth) would rather be writing novels than steering a spaceship.

But for now, my adventurous family and I are busy traveling around the universe on exciting intergalactic missions.

THIS IS THE LATEST ADVENTURE OF THE SPACEMICE!

GALACTIC GORGONZOLA!

It was a calm morning in space aboard the **MouseStar 1**, the most FABUMOUSE spaceship in the universe.

We were traveling at *super-warp* speeds in the far-off CheddaR GalAxy.

I was still asleep in my cabin, snoring blissfully, when **SOMEONE** appeared behind me, sneakily took hold of my blanket, and shouted in a robotic voice:

"Yellow alert! Yellow alert! Yellow alerrrrrt!"

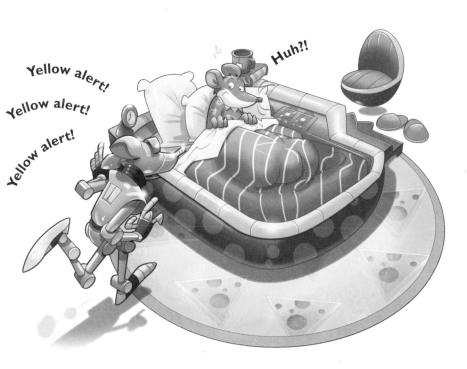

My eyes flew open as if I'd been stung by a swarm of **space bees**.

It was **Assistatrix**, my personal-assistant robot.

"**GALACTIC GORGONZOLA!**" I squeaked. "What is it? What's wrong? Have **aliens** invaded? Did a meteorite hit the spaceship?"

"Good morning, Captain Stiltonix," Assistatrix announced in his metallic voice. "It's seven o'clock, intergalactic time. It's time to get up. Time to get up. **TiMe to Get UP!**"

"**Assistatrix**, how many times have I told you not to wake me up with the yellow alert?" I grumbled. "Couldn't you use a more relaxing alarm, like the *Symphony of the Galaxies*?"

"Negative, Captain," he replied. "The **yellow alert** is the only one that works with you. Now, **Get UP, Get UP, Get UP!**"

A long mechanical arm **extended** from a compartment in Assistatrix's back. The arm grabbed me by the tail and lifted me **uP** like a fish on a hook!

"**Help**!" I squeaked. "Put me down!

4

I'll get ready at the SPEED OF LIGHT— I promise!"

I should have kept my snout shut. A second later, he released me suddenly, and **bam!** I crashed to the ground, smacking my snout against the floor and crushing my whiskers. OUCH!

Sometimes I really wish that the MOUSESTAR 1 didn't have artificial gravity. In zero gravity, I would have just floated away instead of crashing to the floor!

I rubbed my sore whiskers as Assistatrix continued to squeak at me.

"Captain Stiltonix, you're late. Late, late, late! It's time to wash, time to wash, time to wash!"

MARTIAN MOZZARELLA!
He can't treat me that way — I'm the captain of this ship!

OOPS! I haven't introduced myself yet. My name is Stiltonix, Geronimo Stiltonix. I'm the captain of the MouseStar 1, the most fabumouse spaceship in the entire universe!

Assistatrix grabbed me by the tail and pushed me into the Wash-O-Mouse, the ship's space-age shower. As soon as the doors closed, I was hit with a powerful jet of icy water!

"Assistatrix!" I cried, my teeth chattering.

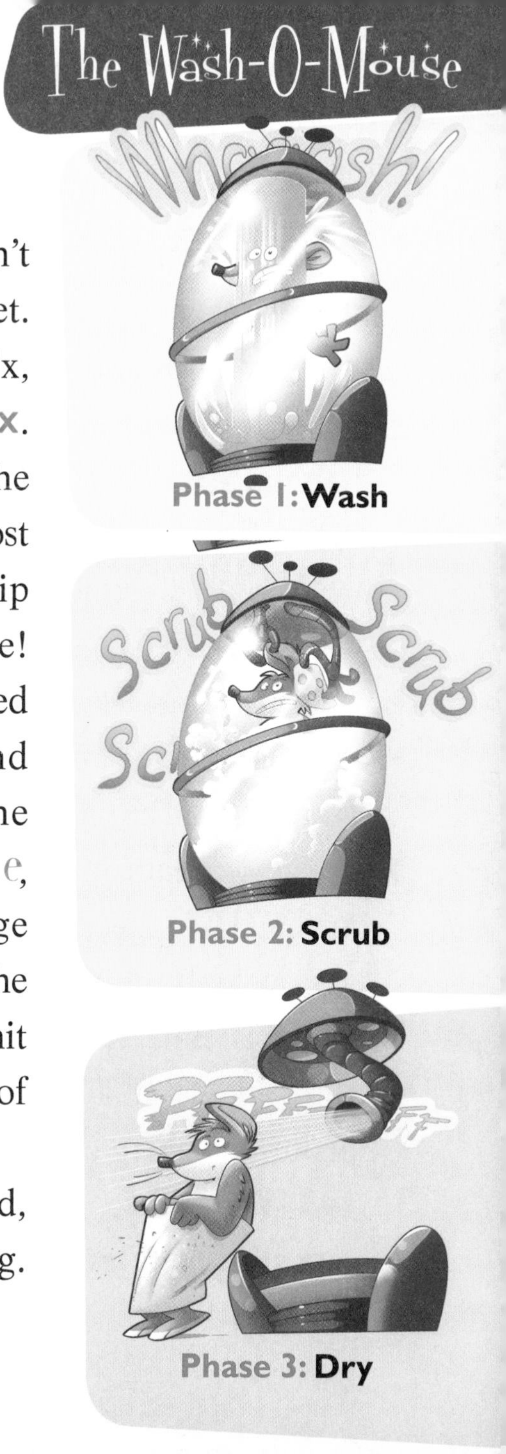
The Wash-O-Mouse
Phase 1: Wash
Scrub
Scrub
Phase 2: Scrub
Phase 3: Dry

"This shower is f~f~freezing!"

But three ROTATING brushes had already grabbed me, **squeezed** me, scrubbed me, polished me, and buffed me.

Finally, I was hit with a *blast* of hot air to fluff up my fur.

"Yeow!" I squeaked. "Assistatrix! This air is boiling hot!"

Why, oh, why was I being subjected to such terrible treatment? I never wanted to be a spaceship captain! My greatest dream in life is actually to become an author. I've always wanted to write a novel about the *adventures* of the spacemice. But I never seem to have the time! I'm always too busy *ZIPPING* around the galaxy as captain of the *MouseStar 1*.

I stumbled out of the Wash-O-Mouse

and **shook** out my fur. Then Assistatrix opened the door to my closet for me.

"Captain Stiltonix, today I recommend you wear your *dress uniform*," Assistatrix said. "There's a control room visit scheduled with the former captain of the ship, the retired admiral, **His Excellency**, the great William Stiltonix."

What? What? What?

Grandfather William is coming?

"**What? What? What?**" I squeaked. "Grandfather William is coming to the control room? Today? Why am I always the last to know? **HELP**!"

I Always Get Spacesick!

"**Get dressed, Get dressed, GET DRESSED!**" Assistatrix continued, handing me my *super-fancy special dress uniform*.

I tried to put it on, but I had gained a little weight since the last time I wore it. Holey space cheese, I couldn't fasten my **belt**!

"Don't worry, Captain," Assistatrix assured me. "I've got it!"

And with that he grabbed me, **spun** me around, **crushed** me, *bashed* me, **smushed** me, and **tugged** on me until finally . . . **CLICK**! My belt was fastened!

I was finally dressed, but I couldn't relax yet.

CAPTAIN STILTONIX'S
SUPER-FANCY SPECIAL DRESS UNIFORM

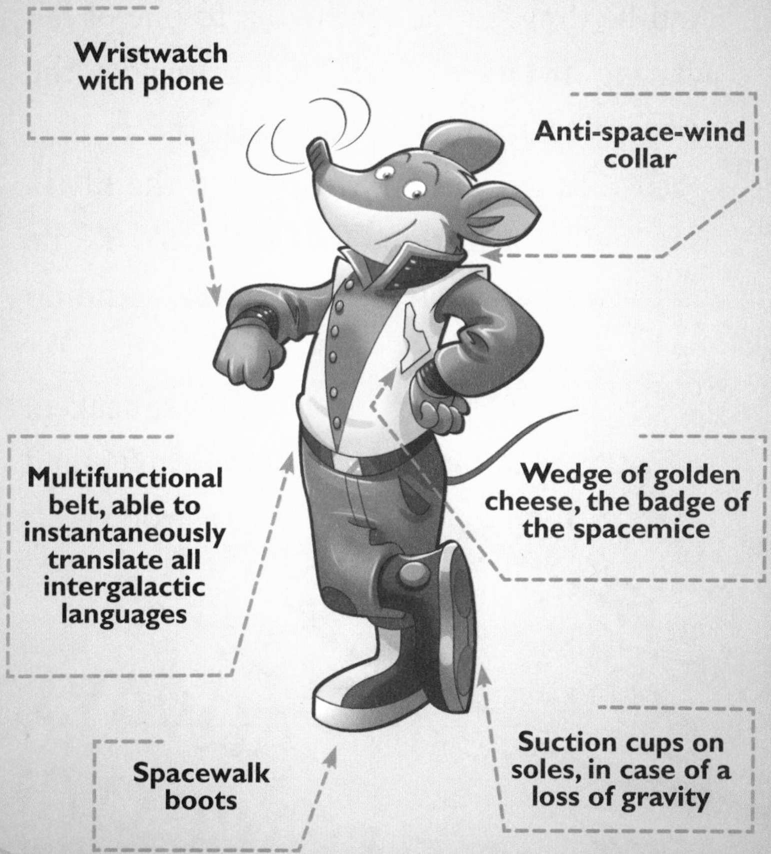

Wristwatch with phone

Anti-space-wind collar

Multifunctional belt, able to instantaneously translate all intergalactic languages

Wedge of golden cheese, the badge of the spacemice

Spacewalk boots

Suction cups on soles, in case of a loss of gravity

"Hurry!" Assistatrix shouted at me. "The **ASTROTAXI** is waiting for you!" And he dragged me by the tail to one of the waiting **mini-ships** that transport the spacemice around the **MOUSESTAR 1**.

"Take Captain Stiltonix to the liftrix elevator to the **CONTROL ROOM**," he ordered the driver. "And do it at **TOP SPEED**!"

"Help!" I squeaked.

"I can't stand astrotaxis.

Get me out of this thing!

I ALWAYS GET SPACESICK!"

But it was too late. The astrotaxi zoomed off and I felt my stomach lurch. Mousey meteorites — I hoped I wouldn't toss my cheese!

Finally, the astrotaxi stopped. I climbed out and **wobbled** toward the liftrix, which is the special elevator that goes to the CONTROL ROOM. Suddenly, I felt someone — or some*thing* — pinch my tail.

It was **Robotix**!

Robotix is a mischievous little robot. He is autoprogrammed, autoregulated, free-floating, and, to be honest, a little annoying. He's convinced he knows everything and that he's always right. He never admits his mistakes, and he always wants to have the last word in every ARGUMENT!

"What's the problem, Captain Stiltonix?" Robotix asked with a giggle. "Are you lost?

Maybe you're looking for the liftrix to get to the control room?"

"I know exactly where I'm going, thank you —" I began, but Robotix cut me off.

"It's okay, **Captain Stiltonix**!" **Robotix** squeaked. "I've always known that you need a lot of help with directions! Follow me!"

I didn't even have **time** to reply before

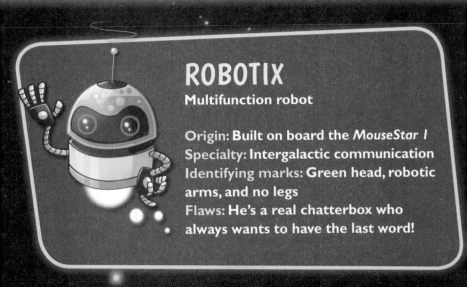

ROBOTIX
Multifunction robot

Origin: **Built on board the *MouseStar I***
Specialty: **Intergalactic communication**
Identifying marks: **Green head, robotic arms, and no legs**
Flaws: **He's a real chatterbox who always wants to have the last word!**

he grabbed me by the **tail** and dragged me toward a **clear** tube.

"Go ahead, get on the liftrix!" he said bossily as he shoved me inside. "Just press the **RED** button for the control room."

"I know, I know!" I replied in exasperation. "I'm the captain of the ship, remember?"

Of course I knew what the **red button** was for!

Suddenly, a powerful **BLAST** of air lifted

me and hurled me upward like a meteor heading straight for the moon.

GALACTIC GORGONZOLA!

Would I ever get used to the liftrix? I always seemed to get spacesick!

Help!

From the Encyclopedia Galactica
LIFTRIX

The liftrix is the fastest and most comfortable way to move around inside a spaceship. It's a glass tube that sucks up the passenger in a strong blast of air, carrying the spacemouse to the requested level of the ship.

ORDERS
ARE ORDERS!

A few moments later, I popped out of the liftrix and into the ship's *CONTROL ROOM*.

My tummy rumbled and I licked my whiskers at the thought of the lunar cheese shake that would be waiting for me at the command chair, as it is every morning. It's my daily breakfast! I hoped my grandfather hadn't arrived yet so I could enjoy my shake in peace.

But before I could even make my way to the command chair, my cousin Trap appeared out of nowhere.

"Geronimo, did you bring some cheese and crackers and a few bottles of fizzy feta-flavored sodas to celebrate our new mission?"

"What NEW MISSION?" I asked. "No one told me we were going on a new mission."

Why am I always the last to know?

Trap shook his head, disappointed.

"Geronimo, I eXPecTeD you to be PREPARED," he said. "What kind of captain are you?"

PREPARED?! How could I be prepared when I was always the last to know what was HAPPENING?! To show him that I was a real captain, I sat down in the COMMAND CHAIR. And to show him that I knew exactly what I was doing, I pressed a bunch of **buttons** on the arm of the chair. I'd never done that before, but it seemed like the right move.

Whoops! Big mistake.

Zip! Zap! Zop!

A set of mechanical arms appeared from beneath the chair. One arm **sprayed** me with a fire extinguisher! Another twisted my tail into a knot! One arm splashed my feet with water! And another offered me a cheese sandwich!

Just then, the door to the control room flew open.

"What in the universe is going on in here?" boomed a voice I knew well. **MARTIAN MOZZARELLA!** My grandfather William — retired captain of the *MOUSESTAR 1* — had arrived! I JUMPED out of my chair to greet him.

Before he even said hello, he pressed a button on the chair that made all the mechanical arms retract. Then he flopped

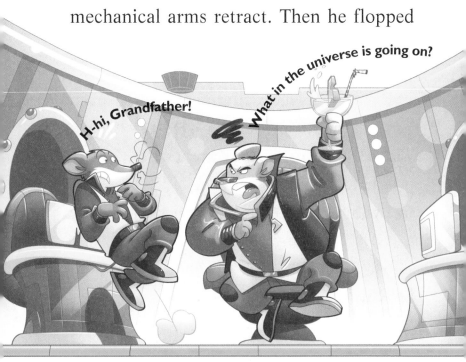

H-hi, Grandfather!

What in the universe is going on?

down in *my* chair, put his **Paws** on *my* pawrests, and started to sip *my lunar cheese shake* as if he had never retired!

"H-hi, Grandfather!" I squeaked. "To what do I owe this, um, *friendly* visit?"

"What do you mean, *friendly* visit?" he yelled, glaring at me. "I'm not just stopping by to say hi. Can't you see that I'm in my high-command UNIFORM? I took the trouble to come down here from my *super-luxurious* cabin because of an extremely serious matter: The **MouseStar 1** is about to explode!"

What? What?! What?!? The **MouseStar 1**, our fabumouse spaceship, was about to **explode**? This was extremely **serious**!

"Why am I always the last to know?" I squeaked.

Grandfather William took three gulps of my shake and SHOOK his head with disapproval. "Because you should already know!" he barked. "But you've always got your head in the STARS, reading and writing science fiction books! I'm beginning to wonder if I should turn the **command** of this ship over to your sister, Thea —"

"Is the *MOUSESTAR 1* really going to explode?" I interrupted. I may not be the best captain, but I didn't want to lose command of my ship!

"Oh, Grandson, do I need to explain everything to you?" he replied impatiently. "Do you know how the **ENGINE** of the ship works?"

"Of course!" I replied indignantly. "Er, the, um, tetrastellar batteries, er, they collect stellar energy and —"

"And what happens when the stellar energy batteries **OVERHEAT**?" Grandfather prompted me.

I hesitated. "Um . . . well, let's see . . . maybe . . . the engine **explodes**?"

"Of course!" He snorted. "And we'll all burn up like a meteor entering the Earth's atmosphere!"

I **shuddered**. I didn't like the idea of **burning up** one bit!

"Luckily, **I'm** here, and **I've** already

From the Encyclopedia Galactica

TETRASTELLIUM

The *MouseStar I* speeds along quickly through the galaxy thanks to powerful batteries made of tetrastellium, an element that is able to last for thousands of centuries. Unfortunately, though, tetrastellium is also very rare. When a long voyage is planned, it's important to have a good supply in case the batteries run low!

found a solution," Grandfather boasted. "We need new batteries so we can stabilize the engine. Unfortunately, though, the **tetrastellium** that powers the batteries is a very rare element, and it exists only on a few planets. But we will find it!"

"Okay, Grandfather, but what do you mean 'we'?" I asked. "Aren't you retired?"

"Geronimo, I gave you command of this ship, and I can also take it away if I want to," he replied.

"But, Grandfather, if you take away my

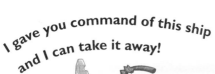

I gave you command of this ship and I can take it away!

command, what will all my friends, all the crew, and all the captains of all the other ships in the universe think of me?"

"Grandson, there must be a *black hole* in your head if you think you can solve a problem this **ENORMOUSE** without some help! While **you** were sleeping, I had already identified a PLANET only three-point-seven light-years away from us that may have tetrastellium: the planet **Rattos**. We're going there immediately!"

"But, Grandfather, I was just about to begin **writing** my novel —" I began, but he cut me off.

"Orders are orders, Grandson!" he commanded. "And I am ordering you to do what I say!"

ONCE IN A BLUE CHEESE MOON

Just then, the door of the control room opened again.

This time, it was my BELOVED nephew Benjamin and his best friend, Bugsy Wugsy. Benjamin rushed toward me.

Benjamin!

"Hi, Uncle Geronimo!" he squeaked. "Can we stay with you in the control room today?" I was just about to reply when a **GREEN** creature covered in **LEAVES** from the tips of his ears to the end of his tail entered the room.

It looked like a walking bush, but I knew it was **PROFESSOR GREENFUR**!

Professor Greenfur comes from the planet Photosyntheson, and he is our official onboard **scientist**. He knows all the species of plants and animals in the entire galaxy! I shook his **Paw**.

"Welcome, Professor," I greeted him. "We could use your help finding the *tetrastellium* that we need to power the **MOUSESTAR 1's** batteries."

"At your service, Captain Stiltonix," Professor Greenfur replied. "Though I'm surprised to hear that we're running low on tetrastellium — it lasts for **CeNTURieS**! It only needs to be replaced once in a

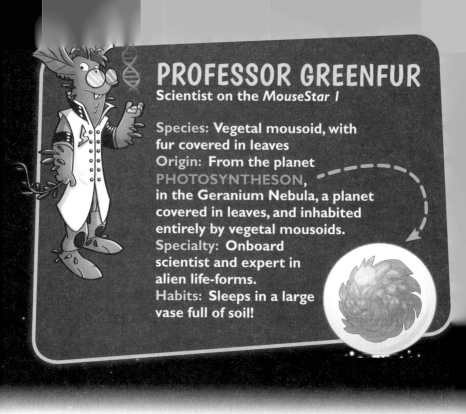

PROFESSOR GREENFUR
Scientist on the *MouseStar 1*

Species: Vegetal mousoid, with fur covered in leaves
Origin: From the planet PHOTOSYNTHESON, in the Geranium Nebula, a planet covered in leaves, and inhabited entirely by vegetal mousoids.
Specialty: Onboard scientist and expert in alien life-forms.
Habits: Sleeps in a large vase full of soil!

BLUE CHEESE MOON. In other words, almost never!"

I nodded. "I know, Professor, but it's true," I explained, trying to sound like a responsible captain. "And if we don't find more tetrastellium soon, the MOUSESTAR 1 will explode!"

"**What?!?**" Benjamin and Bugsy Wugsy exclaimed in unison.

Benjamin looked up at me with **WIDE** eyes.

"Uncle, is it true?" he asked, a **WORRIED** look on his snout. "Are we in **danger**?"

I hugged my little nephew closely. "Of course not!" I told him. "We can leave the **MouseStar 1** in our **space pods** if necessary. But we won't have to do that. I won't be satisfied until our mission to find more tetrastellium is **complete**!"

"Hooray!" Benjamin and Bugsy Wugsy cheered.

Now I just had to make good on my *promise*.

CODE RED!
ALIEN INVASION!

At that moment, I heard a lovely, melodious voice.

"Captain Stiltonix, the engines are ready for *hyperspeed*," the voice said.

I looked up and saw a **rodent** with long, curly **purple** hair; eyes as **blue** as a lunar lake; and an irresistible smile. It was **Sally de Wrench**, the ship's expert in photon circuitry, hyperspace engines, **STELLAR** energy — and the loveliest rodent on the *MOUSESTAR 1*!

"Captain, did you hear me?" she asked. "I need your order to go into *hyperspeed*."

"Um . . . yes, of course, of course!" I

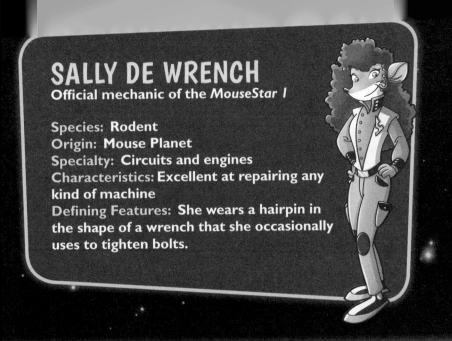

SALLY DE WRENCH
Official mechanic of the *MouseStar I*

Species: Rodent
Origin: Mouse Planet
Specialty: Circuits and engines
Characteristics: Excellent at repairing any kind of machine
Defining Features: She wears a hairpin in the shape of a wrench that she occasionally uses to tighten bolts.

babbled. "Go ahead and fire it up. I mean, LET'S GO!" I tried to sound official and captainlike, but I'm pretty sure I had failed miserably.

The engines started with an ultrasonic BANG.

A moment later, the *MOUSESTAR 1* was heading toward the planet Rattos! We sailed for hours before Sally finally signaled that we were almost there.

"We've arrived in the area near RATTOS!" she said. "DECREASE SPEED!"

We had arrived! Rattos was a large planet with an enormouse pink splotch in the middle of it. The splotch sparkled on our main screen like a gigantic splat of

strawberry ice cream.

I didn't have time to celebrate our arrival, though, because **suddenly** a hideous beast appeared next to my chair. It was all teeth, antennae, and tentacles.

"**AHHHHH**!" I squeaked. "**Code red! Alien invasion!**"

Start the engines!

Suddenly, the beast started laughing. Then it took off its **MASK** and I saw that it was my cousin Trap.

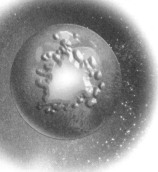

"**Ha, ha, ha!**" Trap laughed. "I really got you that time, Geronimo! Oh, how I love playing jokes on you! I gave you a real scare, didn't I, Cuz?"

"You did," I replied. "But **WHY** would you do that to me?"

I should have been able to guess Trap's response.

"Isn't it obvious?" he asked. "I'm just trying to keep you on the **tips** of your paws! Our grandfather, **ADMIRAL WILLIAM**, told me to keep an eye on you. I'm supposed to make sure you're always **awake, alert,** and **ready** for anything, and I'm carrying out his $\mathscr{ORDERS}$!"

Mousey meteorites!

Why me?

"After all, I'm your second-in-command!" Trap continued. "Don't you see the yellow uniform I'm wearing? It's the uniform of a lieutenant. **Lieutenant Trap Stiltonix**. Sounds good, doesn't it?"

Then he gave me a giant clap on the shoulder.

Like my joke?

Ahhhhh!

Monster mask

"Come on, Cousin!" he said. "Before we land on this planet, let's have a SNACK together in the cafeteria. Your treat, naturally!"

My stomach grumbled. Since Grandfather William had stolen my lunar cheese shake, I had skipped breakfast. I was really, really hungry.

We arrived at the Space Yum Café, and I looked over the day's menu. I was squeakless! The specials were Plutonian stone soup with lichens, toasted moss from Sprinx, and spicy seaweed pie à la Croz.

"Black holey galaxies!" I squeaked. "This food isn't for mice. . . . It's for space rocks!"

"Shhh!" Trap said. "Don't let the new cook hear you. He's very SENSiTiVE!"

The new cook was an orange creature with tentacles, claws, arms, three eyes, and an apron speckled with mysterious fluorescent stains.

"Hello, Captain. I'm SQUIZZY, the ship's new cook," he introduced himself. "Please make yourself comfortable. I can't wait for you to taste all the fantastic alien specialties that I can make!"

"Um, actually, I'm not very hungry today," I said.

But Cook SQUIZZY wouldn't back down. "I insist, Captain!" he said. "Please sit down. I'll serve you in a moment!"

"But he didn't even take our orders!" I whispered to Trap. "How does he know what I want?"

"It's obvious, Cuz!" Trap replied. "He

doesn't! But our grandfather, **ADMIRAL WILLIAM**, told him you haven't been eating enough healthy foods lately. So you're on a seaweed-only meal plan! I, on the other hand, will have a nice CHEDDAR shake with **chocolate** space sprinkles, as usual."

COOK SQUIZZY
MouseStar I's onboard cook

Species: Alien
Origin: Comes from the planet Brie
Specialties: Experimental fine cuisine
Characteristics: He believes he's a great chef.
Defining Features: He has two arms, two claws, two tentacles, two wings, and three eyes!

"**MARTIAN MOZZARELLA!**"
I squeaked. "I want a CHEDDAR shake
with **chocolate** space sprinkles,
too!"

But the cook **interrupted** me.

"Here you are!" Squizzy said. "I've made
you a soup out of blue seaweed from Vega.
It's very healthy! Admiral
William's orders!"

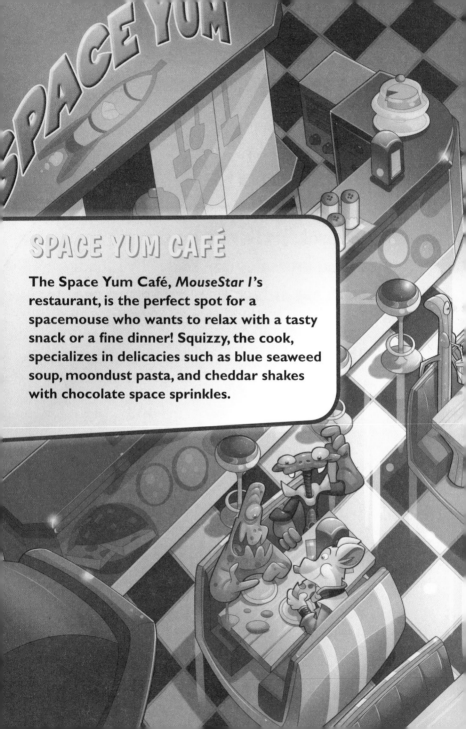

SPACE YUM CAFÉ

The Space Yum Café, *MouseStar I*'s restaurant, is the perfect spot for a spacemouse who wants to relax with a tasty snack or a fine dinner! Squizzy, the cook, specializes in delicacies such as blue seaweed soup, moondust pasta, and cheddar shakes with chocolate space sprinkles.

A REAL LIVE YELLOW ALERT!

Suddenly, a siren went off and a robotic voice shouted:

"Yellow alert! Yellow alert! Yellow alerrrrrt!"

HOLEY CRATERS! That wasn't Assistatrix's alarm clock — it was a real live **yellow alert**!

"What's going on?" I shouted.

A tiny yellow light started to spin around me. It grew and **grew** and **grew**, until a hologram* of a rodent's face appeared right in front of my snout. And it was completely YELLOW!

It was **Hologramix**, our trusty onboard

* A hologram is a three-dimensional image projected by a light source.

computer! Its hologram is programmed to appear wherever it's needed.

"There's an **emergency**, Captain Stiltonix," Hologramix told me. "You must go to the control room immediately!"

"But what's going on?" I asked again. "Can't you **tell me** before we get to the control room?"

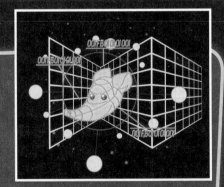

HOLOGRAMIX
MouseStar I's onboard computer

Species: Ultra-advanced artificial intelligence
Specialty: Controls all functions on the ship, including the autopilot function
Characteristics: Considers itself to be indispensable
Defining Features: Appears wherever and whenever it's needed

Hologramix shook its head. "I am authorized to communicate SECRET information only in the control room!"

So I *hurried* toward the liftrix and hopped inside. Then I pushed the red button as QUICKLY as I could, but NOTHING HAPPENED!

"In the case of a yellow alert, the liftrix is shut down," Hologramix reminded me. "You must use physical energy to transport yourself."

I was confused. "Physical energy?" I asked.

"Use the STAIRS!" it explained, rolling its eyes.

Then it disappeared like a Puff of moondust in the wind.

SALUTATIONS, RODENTS!

Getting to the control room using **physical energy** was more exhausting than I thought it would be.

I went up **stairs, stairs**, and more **stairs**, until I finally arrived in the control room. I was drenched in sweat, **short of breath**, and my tongue was hanging out.

Trap didn't lose the chance to make a joke at my expense.

"Cousin, you've got to work out more!" he chided me. "You're slower than a **super-lazy astroslug**. On the other paw, I'm in great shape. I exercise in the ship's **technogym** every morning!"

"Be quiet, you two!" Thea squeaked. "Hologramix needs to communicate with us!"

Hologramix's **bright yellow** face floated in the center of the control room.

"Captain, we've received an alien communication!" Hologramix said.

Galactic gorgonzola! My whiskers trembled with fright.

"The message came from the planet Rattos," Hologramix continued. "Speaking of Rattos, I've made a few calculations to determine the size of the planet's **orbit**. According to the *proton velocity*, the size in quantum photons is —"

Robotix snorted under his breath.

"What a planetary pain," he grumbled. "Hologramix thinks it knows EVERYTHING just because it's a **supercomputer**!"

Unfortunately, Hologramix heard him.

"How dare you insult me, you hunk of **scrap metal**!" Hologramix replied. "I am the most advanced form of electronic

How dare you?!

intelligence ever produced, and I have the most sophisticated PROGRAMMING of all time."

At that point, I jumped in. "Um, excuse me, Hologramix, but we don't have time for arguments!" I explained. "Now, please give us the message from Rattos."

Hologramix transmitted the video message and three strange creatures appeared on the control room's computer screen.

"Greetings, intrepid space travelers!" the figures said. "We are pink mousoids from the planet Rattos!"

The creatures had a mousoid shape, meaning they looked like mice — but they were completely pink!

PROFESSOR GREENFUR scratched the leaves on his head thoughtfully. "Hmm,"

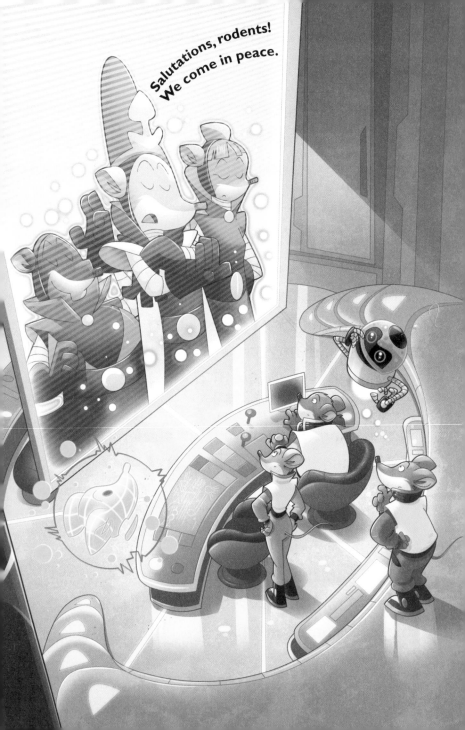

he muttered. "Very strange. I'm not familiar with this Alien population."

One of the pink mousoids waved a hand in greeting.

"Salutations!" she said. "We come in peace, honorable rodents of the *MouseStar 1*! We know that your spaceship is in danger, and we are here to help. We can give you the precious *tetrastellium* that you need."

"This is a real stroke of luck, Geronimo!" Trap exclaimed. "If they help us, the **MISSION** to find more tetrastellium will be completed before it's even started. We should organize a galactic banquet to celebrate!"

Hmm. It sounded like we were saved, but there was something strange about those pink mousoids. It all seemed too easy!

A WHISKERED WELCOME

We invited our new mousoid friends onto the *MouseStar 1*.

I was practically JUMPING out of my fur with nerves. How should we welcome our guests? I didn't want to be RUDE!

"We could give them a gift of a can of precious **super-concentrated oil**," Sally suggested. "It's great for space motors!"

"No, we should give them a nice clump of rotting manure that they can use in their greenhouses!" Professor Greenfur said.

"No, no, no!" Trap countered.

"I know just what they'll want! I'll tell **COOK SQUIZZY** to make one of his specialties. But no seaweed! And no moss. Just high-quality cheese."-->

"The pink mousoids' ship has just entered our hangar!" Hologramix announced.

I *HURRIED* to receive them, and everyone followed me.

The pink mousoids made a formal bow. Then the **tallest** one, who seemed to be the leader, pointed to a floating sphere.

"This *gift* of tetrastellium is a sign of intergalactic friendship," he said.

The sphere opened and a **MYSTERIOUS bOX** appeared right in front of us. It was filled to the brim with a shining **pink** substance!

I cleared my throat.

"Er, thank you friends, but maybe you're mistaken," I said. "I'm afraid this isn't *tetrastellium*.

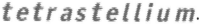

Tetrastellium isn't pink — it's **blue**!"

The tallest pink mousoid stepped forward.

"My rodent friend, you're right," he explained. "Tetrastellium is usually blue, but this is a very rare pink variety. Don't worry: It's absolutely the same as blue tetrastellium! It works GREAT!"

The tall pink mousoid stepped closer to me and narrowed his eyes.

"You'll see that this pink tetrastellium

will be very good for your spaceship," he said. "In fact, it will be *perfect*!"

I turned to PROFESSOR GREENFUR, who was examining the contents of the box with his portable super-detector.

"The sensors have confirmed it with **NINETY-NINE-POINT-NINE-NINE-NINE-NINE-PERCENT** certainty," the professor announced to us. "This is **tetrastellium**!"

Then he shook his head and whispered softly under his breath: "It's so strange, though. I never knew there was a **pink** variety!"

Different Planet, Different Customs

"We're happy to be able to help you!" the tallest pink mousoid said solemnly. "If you stay in orbit around our planet **TONIGHT**, we'll give you another box full of tetrastellium tomorrow! For free!"

I COULDN'T BELIEVE MY EARS!

They were being so generous!

"Thank you so much, honorable pink mousoids from the planet Rattos," I replied ceremoniously. "Our — ahem — very talented cook **SQUIZZY** has prepared one of his cheese specialties for you. Would you like to join us for a banquet?"

"Yeah!" Trap added. "We even have a tasting *menu*!"

Out of the corner of my eye, I noticed that my sister, Thea, was strangely SILENT. She was watching the pink mousoids SUSPICIOUSLY, as if she didn't trust them.

The pink mousoids refused our invitation. "Thank you, dear friends, but we would like to return to our planet as soon as possible," the tall mousoid replied. "We have, um . . . certain business to attend to." **Hmm . . .**

They were just starting to board their ship when Thea stopped them.

"It's very generous of you to give us this precious **tetrastellium** without receiving anything in return," she said.

"We are happy to **HELP**," the tallest pink mousoid replied.

"That's very nice," Thea said, still eyeing them suspiciously. "But are you sure you don't want anything at all in exchange for the tetrastellium?"

The pink mousoids looked offended.

"For us, tetrastellium has no **value** other than friendship!" the tall mousoid replied.

"Yes, we just want to be your **friends**!" the other two mousoids exclaimed in **unison**.

"It's getting late and we really need to go!" the tall mousoid said. "Don't go away, though. We'll bring you **MORE** tetrastellium tomorrow!"

With that, they threw open the doors to their pink spaceship in a **RUSH**. A moment later, they **took off**.

"Such strange pink mousoids," I murmured.

"It's really **true** what Grandfather William always says: **Different planet, different customs.**"

Thea remained **SILENT**, which was very unlike her.

Meanwhile, Trap was muttering to himself through a mouthful of cheese.

"It's a real shame that those pink mousoids didn't taste this cheese," he mumbled. "Oh well, seeing as they've left, I'll take one for the team and eat it. **YUM**!"

SSWOOOSSSH

Professor Greenfur continued to scratch the leaves on his head in **confusion**.

"The data on the tetrastellium is correct, but there's still something **weird** going on!" he muttered. "I've never heard of pink tetrastellium before, and I've studied it for years!"

I also had a strange feeling, but I brushed it off and congratulated myself on how well everything had gone. Our mission was basically **complete**! I couldn't wait to return to my cabin and start writing my *novel*.

RECON MISSION TO RATTOS

During dinner, I told Grandfather William what had happened. Once he learned that we had already found the *tetrastellium*, he actually *complimented* me. I couldn't believe my ears!

"Nice work, Grandson!" he said. "Since the mission is complete, we'll leave tomorrow morning."

I went to sleep that night feeling **great**. But a little after midnight, there was a knock at my door. It was my sister, Thea.

"Psst, Geronimo!" she whispered. "**Wake up!** We need to get to the hangar right away!"

"What?" I replied. "**Why?**"

"No questions. Just **hurry**!" she said.

When my sister gets something in her head, there's **No WaY** to change her mind. So I got up quickly and went out into the hallway.

"**HEY!**" a voice squeaked in the **dArk**. "Who's stepping on my roots?"

"Oops!" I replied. "Sorry! Is that you, Professor Greenfur? I can't see as far as my **whiskers**!"

"I turned off the lights in this area so that the **CREW** can continue to sleep peacefully," Thea explained.

"Yeah, and dream of cheese, like I was doing before you **woke** me," Trap grumbled.

He was here, too! But **why?**

"Shhh!" Thea whispered. "We have a mission to complete."

"B-but I'm a scientist, not a **HERO**!"

Professor Greenfur protested. "I'm not trained to go on a mission to an unknown **planet**! What if I get attacked by aphids, or the climate **DRIES** out my leaves?"

But Thea wasn't swayed.

"We can use a scientist on our team," she said. "And you could stand to see a little **ACTION**!"

"Unknown planet?!" I squeaked. "Thea, **what in the galaxy** is going on?"

But my sister just pushed me into a space pod and started the engine.

"Batteries at full charge, engine in hyperdrive, all **rotors** working," Thea announced. "Let's go!"

"But where are we going, Thea?" I asked again. "And **why**?"

"Oh, stop your squeaking, Geronimo!" Thea replied. "It's no big deal.

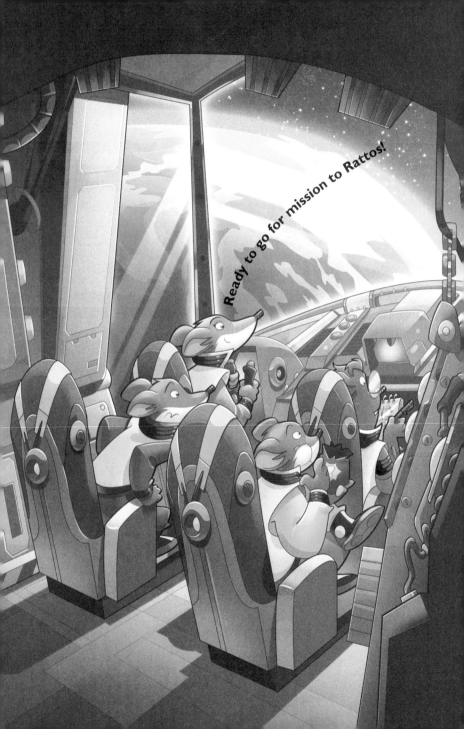

We're just taking a little reconnaissance trip to the **planet Rattos**. I have some SUSPICIONS about those pink mousoids."

Professor Greenfur nodded. "There IS something odd about them," he agreed. "Even their tetrastellium is strange. I studied it closely and it seems authentic, but there's still something off about that pink variety."

"Shouldn't we let Grandfather know our plan?" I squeaked, WORRIED. "Or tell someone else what we're doing?"

"Too late, Geronimo!" Thea replied. "In three . . . two . . . one, we're landing on the **planet Rattos**, right next to that pink **blob** of a lake!"

MILK MISSION!

Meanwhile, Benjamin was tossing and turning in his bed.

A glass of milk *would help!* he thought.

With his wrist phone, he called Bugsy Wugsy. Maybe she couldn't sleep, either.

"Bugsy Wugsy," he whispered. "Are you still up?"

"Yes!" she replied. "I've counted all the constellations, but I still can't fall asleep!"

"What do you say we *GO* find some milk?" Benjamin suggested.

"Yesss!" his friend cried. "Meet you in the hallway in **two minutes**!"

Benjamin padded out of his room, trying not to make any noise. The *MouseStar 1* was

completely silent. Benjamin and Bugsy Wugsy headed toward the **kitchen** together.

"Wait!" Bugsy Wugsy said suddenly. "Did you hear that?"

Benjamin shook his head. "No, I didn't hear **anything**," he replied. "Come on, the refrigerator is right over here. We need to carry out our **milk mission**!"

Bam! Bam! Bam! Clang! Clang! Clang!

Benjamin had knocked into an entire pile of pots and pans! He and Bugsy Wugsy **froze** in their tracks.

They heard a sleepy voice grumbling.

"**Zzzzzz** . . . less salt in that space-ant pie . . ."

It was **SQUIZZY**, the cook. He had fallen asleep right in front of the fridge!

"Now what do we do?" Bugsy Wugsy asked, **disappointed**. "We'll never get the milk out of the fridge without him hearing us."

"What about the pantry?" Benjamin suggested. "There's extra cheese there!"

The two friends walked on the tips of their paws so that they wouldn't wake Squizzy. They headed toward the pantry, which was full of supplies from the most remote galaxies.

Less salt...

"Oh, look!" Bugsy Wugsy exclaimed. "There's gorgonzola from Sirius over here."

"And there are spicy cheeses from Pluto over here!" Benjamin replied.

Suddenly, Benjamin noticed something else in the pantry.

"**Look!**" he whispered. "There's someone over there."

He pointed to a **dArk** corner.

Bugsy Wugsy turned, but she didn't see anyone.

"Where?" Bugsy Wugsy asked. "There's no one there, Benjamin. You must have just seen a **SHADOW**."

"No, I'm sure," Benjamin replied. "**Look!** There's something **pink** moving back there."

Bugsy Wugsy gasped.

"You're right!" she replied. "**WHAT** could it be?"

"We should tell Uncle Geronimo," Benjamin said. "Quick, let's go!"

NOT ANOTHER WORD!

Benjamin and Bugsy Wugsy *ran* to my cabin.

KNOCK! KNOCK! KNOCK!

There was no response. They tried knocking harder, but there was still NO ANSWER!

Then they knocked on Thea's cabin door.

KNOCK! KNOCK! KNOCK!

But there was NO RESPONSE there, either! Finally, they knocked on Trap's cabin door.

KNOCK! KNOCK! KNOCK!

There was NO REPLY! Where was everyone? It was very, very strange!

Benjamin tried to contact each of us using

his **wrist phone**. But he just heard an electronic voice:

"Unreachable, unreachable, unreachable!"

"Rat-munching robots!" Benjamin exclaimed. "What's going on?

He and Bugsy Wugsy went up to the control room.

As soon as they entered, **Robotix** woke up.

"Good morning, everyone!" he exclaimed **LOUDLY**.

"Shhh!" Benjamin whispered. "It's still nighttime!"

"So why did you wake me up?" Robotix replied. "I was *dreaming* about

Why did you wake me up?

Shhh!

an exciting, top secret mission in spa —"

"We need your help!" Benjamin explained, interrupting him. "Can you CONTACT my uncle Geronimo? Or my aunt Thea?"

"Of course I can!" Robotix scoffed. "That's so EASY for me! Wait just two astroseconds."

Robotix began to *fiddle* with dozens of colorful buttons until the large screen in the center of the control room turned on. Benjamin and Bugsy Wugsy watched as our space pod landed on the pink planet. A second later, I climbed out, followed by Thea, Trap, and Professor Greenfur.

"Uncle Geronimo, Aunt Thea, **where are you**?" Benjamin asked.

"Benjamin?" Thea replied. "We're . . . *bip bip bip* . . . landing on the surface . . . *bip bip bip* . . . of the planet Rattos.

There are . . . *bip bip bip —*"

But the transmission was **interrupted** before she could finish her sentence.

A huge mass of **pink** goo had suddenly appeared in the control room. The blob of goo oozed onto the control panel, shutting the screen down.

Not another word!

"Not another word, you little **troublemakers**!" the enormouse pink blob gurgled **evilly**.

Watch Out for the Great Blob!

Come in, MouseStar 1!

Meanwhile, on the **pink** surface of the planet Rattos, Thea repeatedly tried to call the *MouseStar 1*.

"Come in, *MouseStar 1*," she said. "Come in!"

But there was NO REPLY.

"Someone has interrupted our communication feed," Thea said, looking CONCERNED.

"We're heading back to the ship immediately!" I told my sister. "Benjamin and Bugsy Wugsy could be in DANGER! And we may be in danger, too!"

But Trap didn't want to hear it.

"Relax, Cousin," he said. "You **worry** too much! And you grumble more than a **Grumbloid tragicus**! Benjamin and Bugsy Wugsy are smart mouselets. They'll be fine. And as for us, what dangerous thing do you think is happening on this planet? There's **nothing** here but rocks, bushes, and that weird **pink** lake."

Trap had barely finished speaking when the **pink** water suddenly came to life!

"Out of my way, you balls of fur!" it said. **GALACTIC GORGONZOLA!**

Had the lake really just **talked**? Before I could figure out what was going on, the lake began slithering **right toward us**!

My whiskers **trembled** with fright!

The **pink** lake came closer and spoke again. "What are you doing on **my** planet, you scrawny little furballs?"

Trap, Professor Greenfur, and I **fearfully** backed up.

Only Thea stood her ground.

"See, Geronimo?" she said. "I knew there was something strange about this planet!"

"But . . . but . . . what kind of creature are you?" Professor Greenfur asked in a voice that **trembled** like a leaf.

The **gooey mass** laughed wildly.

"Ha, ha, ha!" he said gleefully. "I am the **Great Blob**! I bet you didn't know what was happening, right? I'll explain it to

you, you silly mice! There's no such thing as pink mousoids! The ones you met on your spaceship were parts of me! HA, HA, HA! I, the **Great Blob**, have the power to transform myself into anything. I can even separate pieces of my **IMMENSE** body, and they may look different, but they are still part of me!"

Mousey meteorites! I was squeakless with fright.

"Of course!" exclaimed Professor Greenfur as he slapped his forehead in disbelief. Unlike me, he understood everything. "You are a fluid and shape-shifting life-form!"

"Ha, ha, ha!" The **Great Blob** bragged, "Exactly! I sent pieces of myself up to your spaceship in the form of

pink tetrastellium. Then in the middle of the night, the tetrastellium **MORPHED** and escaped, and now it's taken control of your ship! *Oh, I am so, so wicked!*"

"But how is that possible?!" I exclaimed. "*You don't believe me?*" he replied. "Look, cheesebrain! See how I transformed into pink mousoids!"

With that, the Great Blob momentarily took the shape of the pink mousoids who had brought the pink tetrastellium to the *MouseStar 1*. Then, just as quickly, he turned back into a pink puddle.

"But why do you want to **TAKE CONTROL** of our spaceship?" Thea asked.

"Because this planet is **boring, boring, boring**!" The Great Blob gurgled. "I want a powerful spaceship like yours so I can get out of here. I'll invade every **GALAXY** in the **UNiVERSE**, and I'll continue to transform myself until the whole universe is populated only by **ME**!"

I shuddered. What a horrible thought!

"You'll never do it!" Thea cried. "We'll stop you!"

"And how do you plan to stop me, you miserable little rodents?"

"Don't underestimate us!" my sister replied. "The universe is full of danger, but there are lots of good creatures out there, too — and many are our FRIENDS!"

The Great Blob just laughed. "Perhaps these FRIENDS of yours exist, but they'll never find you," he cackled. "And do you know why? Because you will stay imprisoned here forever!"

WHOOSH! WHOOSH! BOING!

Meanwhile, on the *MouseStar 1*, the gooey pink monster grabbed Benjamin and Bugsy Wugsy by their tails.

"I am the Great Blob!" he shouted. "No more questions, you nosy little mouselets!"

Hologramix suddenly appeared in the control room. *"What's going on here?"*

Benjamin and Bugsy Wugsy used the distraction to **free** themselves from the pink blob.

"Let's get out here!" Bugsy Wugsy yelled.

The Great Blob *chased* them through the hallways of the *MouseStar 1*.

"Quick, let's **SQUEEZE** into the air ducts!" Benjamin suggested.

Robotix helped them unscrew the air vent. Then Benjamin, Bugsy Wugsy, and the little robot squeezed into the spaceship's slippery metal pipes. **Whoosh! Whoosh! Boing!**

"Wow!" Benjamin squeaked. "This is better than the **SLIDES** at Astral Park!"

"Maybe, but I'm getting covered in **dents**!"

THE *MOUSESTAR 1*'S
AIR DUCTS

Ohhhh!

Ahhhh!

the robot grumbled.

The three found themselves in a **dark** storage room.

"Where are we?" Bugsy Wugsy asked. "I can't **SEE** anything."

Robotix quickly rearranged his bolts. "I've got it!" he replied. A moment later, the robot's eyes *lit up* like two lamps.

"What is this place?" Benjamin asked, looking around.

The storage room was full of large **CRATES**.

"We're in the storeroom for the spaceship's **SPARE PARTS**," Robotix explained.

Suddenly, they heard a strange sound coming from one of the large crates: **Tock! Tock! Tock!**

Robotix tapped the crate with his robotic arm: **Tick! Tick! Tick!**

Immediately, there was a response: **Tock! Tock! Tock!**

Bugsy Wugsy grew impatient. "Robotix, please, stop all that

tick, tick, ticking and **tock, tock, tocking**: The Great Blob will find us!"

"I'm not the one going **tock, tock, tock**!" Robotix replied.

Suddenly, there was a voice from *INSIDE* the crate.

"Help!" the voice squeaked. "Get me out of here!"

It was **Sally de Wrench**!

Robotix extended his robotic hammer and chisel, and a moment later, he had **opened** the crate.

Sally jumped out. "Finally!" she shouted.

"**WHAT HAPPENED?**" Benjamin asked, shocked.

"I've been shut in there for hours," Sally explained. "After dinner, I was in my cabin getting ready for bed when an **enormouse pink gooey blob** attacked me and shut me up in this crate."

But before she could finish her story, the **STOREROOM** door was suddenly flung open.

PRISONERS OF THE GREAT BLOB!

It was the Great Blob!

"Surrender!" the gooey pink monster exclaimed. "You are prisoners of the **Great Blob!**"

Sally turned to Benjamin and Bugsy Wugsy.

"Quick!" she said. "Over there is some superglue that I use to fix the spaceship. Maybe we can use it to glue down the monster and **IMMOBILIZE** him!"

"**Ha, ha, ha!**" the Great Blob gurgled. "It's not that easy to **capture** me!"

Suddenly, the pink blob spread out, growing **LARGER** and **LARGER** until it finally divided into hundreds of **tiny** identical parts that slid around the spaceship's floor and disappeared in an instant.

"Where did he go?" Benjamin asked, confused. "He couldn't have **dissolved** into nothing!"

Robotix **floated** around, inspecting every corner of the room. Then he gasped.

"Look!" he cried. *"The fire extinguisher is moving . . . and it's pink!"*

Suddenly, the pink fire extinguisher started to quickly **BOUNCE** out into the hallway.

Boing! Boing! Boing!

"Doesn't that control panel seem a little **pink**, too?" Benjamin asked.

A second later, the control panel **melted** into a pink puddle and slid away.

"The Great Blob has divided into many small parts and then **transformed** into the objects in this room!" Bugsy Wugsy exclaimed.

Sally didn't waste a second. "It will be difficult to CAPTURE all the Blob parts, but we have to try," she said. "Come on, let's search every corner of this spaceship! When you see a piece of the Great Blob, squirt it with superglue to **immobilize** it!"

And so the group armed themselves with superglue and started to search the ship for every piece of the Great Blob.

In the bathroom, a strangely **pink** sink made a face at Benjamin and quickly escaped right before his eyes.

In the hallway, a pink doorknob grabbed Bugsy Wugsy by the tail. Luckily, Benjamin sprayed the doorknob with **superglue**, saving Bugsy from being captured by the Great Blob.

In the control room, a **pink chair** tried to bite poor Robotix. The Great Blob also transformed into buttons, monitors, and cables that cried out all together: **"This ship belongs to the Great Blob!"**

From the Encyclopedia Galactica
SUPERGLUE

Superglue is an indispensable tool for every spacemouse and should always be kept at close paw's reach. It can fix (almost) anything, from broken vases to cracked spaceship windows to Robotix's metal parts to the holographic screen in the control room. It can also be used to immobilize blobby pink aliens from the planet Rattos!

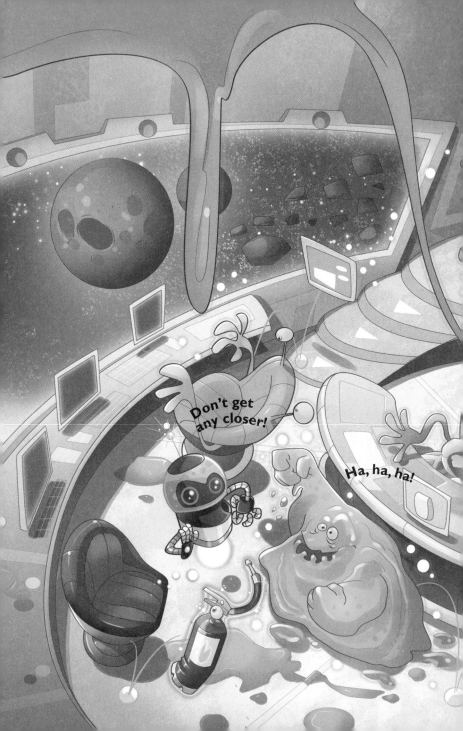

I Challenge You!

Meanwhile, on the planet Rattos, the **Great Blob** had claimed victory over me, Thea, Trap, and Professor Greenfur.

"I WIN!" the Great Blob cackled. "Your spaceship is already mine!"

"How do you know that?" I asked. "Communication with the *MouseStar 1* is down."

The Great Blob burst out laughing. "**Ha, ha, ha!**" he cackled. "I am here, but I am also there. I am wherever there's a drop of my pink **goo**. Soon I will leave you four behind on this **boring** planet and take your spaceship to **conquer the universe**!"

I felt like the **WORST** captain in intergalactic history! I had failed my mission and I was about to lose the *MouseStar 1*.

Professor Greenfur was sweating rivers of sap from nerves.

Thea was **shaking** with anger.

Trap, on the other paw, had come up with a shrewd plan.

"So, Great Blob, would you say that you're a **CHAMPION** at transformation?" Trap asked the glob of goo.

"Of course!" the Great Blob proclaimed **PROUDLY**, puffing up his blobby pink chest. "No one in the universe is better than me!"

"Then I challenge you!" Trap exclaimed.

I was shocked. What in space was my cousin up to?

The **Great Blob** also seemed surprised.

But Trap continued. "Let's really see what kind of transformation you can do," he said. Then he **GRINNED** sneakily. "You say you're so good, Great Blob, but you haven't shown us anything truly **impressive** yet! What do you say? Do you accept my challenge, or are you afraid to fail?"

1. Alien plant

2. Comet

Easy!

Boring!

"Just watch, you impertinent mouse!" the Great Blob thundered, insulted.

A moment later, he showed us a series of **transformations**. He became:

1. a strange alien **plant** . . .
2. a **comet** with a long tail, and . . .
3. a gigantic **dinosaur**!

3. Dinosaur from the Cretacix Galaxy

Is that it?

"So?!" the Great Blob asked proudly. "Is that **impressive** enough for you?"

Trap yawned. "Is that it?"

"What do you mean, 'IS THAT IT?'!" the Great Blob replied angrily.

"That was nothing!" Trap explained. "You're the one who **chose** what you transformed into! But to show us that you're truly great, you must **transform** into what I choose!"

I HAD NO IDEA WHAT TRAP WAS UP TO, BUT I HOPED IT WAS SOMETHING GOOD!

A Superstellar Contest

The Great Blob seemed to be on the brink of LOSING HIS PATIENCE.

"Miserable mice, now you've really ANNOYED me!" he thundered threateningly.

My whiskers trembled with **fear**! But Trap stood his ground.

"Impertinent mouse, how dare you challenge me?" the Great Blob said to Trap. "Tell me what shape you want me to take! Then you'll see that there's nothing I can't imitate, because I am the **Great Blob**!"

My *fur* stood on end. The Great Blob

was really FURIOUS! How had I gotten into this mess? I never asked to become the *captain* of a spaceship. I never asked to go on a MISSION to an alien planet. I always wanted to be a quiet *novelist*! And why, oh, why did my cousin have to continue to annoy this gigantic, scary blob of a creature?

Yum!

Meanwhile, Trap calmly took a box of cheesy mints out of his pocket. He emptied all but one mint into his mouth and polished them off with one giant GULP.

"You've transformed yourself into things that are huge, but can you change into something as small as this piece of candy?" Trap asked the Great Blob, showing him the tiny mint.

The **Great Blob** seemed angrier than ever.

"Of course I can do that!" he shouted.

"But can you fit **all** of yourself — and I mean every last drop of you — in this box?" Trap asked. "I'm not sure you can!"

The Great Blob threw his gooey mouth open and laughed. "**Ha, ha, ha!**" he said. "Is that it? That's such an **easy** challenge. In fact, that's the **easiest** challenge in the entire **UNIVERSE**!"

And with that he made himself **smaller** and **smaller**, till he was the smallest we had seen him yet. Then he called back all the little pieces of **goo** that were on the *MouseStar 1* and made them so **tiny** that a moment later, he was just a minuscule pink dot. Finally, he squeezed himself into the box!

"See? I win!" he said from **inside** the box. "**ALL** of me, and I mean every last drop of me, is in here!"

Then, *FASTER* than a shooting star, Trap closed the box.

Snap!

Quick-thinking Thea took out a tube of superglue and glued the box **shut** so the Great Blob could **never**, **ever** get out.

We were SAVED!

Spacemice for One, Spacemice for All

"Hooray!" we shouted together. "We've defeated the **Great Blob**!"

We were preparing to return to the *MouseStar 1* when Professor Greenfur noticed **something** in the bottom of the lake where the Great Blob had been just minutes before.

"Look!" the professor cried. He pointed to the empty lake. We could see a **crack** in the dry ground. And in the crack was a large deposit of *tetrastellium*!

Professor Greenfur analyzed the deposit with his portable SUPER-DETECTOR.

"Captain Stiltonix, I can confirm that

this is tetrastellium, and it's completely pure!" he finally concluded.

I let out a *sigh* of relief and thanked my **lucky stars**: We would be able to save the *MouseStar 1* from destruction after all!

"Quick, to the spaceship!" I cried.

We flew back to the *MouseStar 1* *faster than the speed of light*, taking

A deposit of pure tetrastellium!

a very precious and **HEAVY** load of *tetrastellium* with us!

We had to move quickly. We had no idea how much longer the tetrastellar batteries would last!

As soon as I got back to the control room, I gave Sally the tetrastellium and asked her to switch out the tetrastellar batteries.

Then I thanked Trap for his **QUICK** thinking.

"Cousin, that was truly amazing!" I told him.

"Thanks!" he replied proudly. "And now, how about we celebrate with an enormouse cheese b a n q u e t?"

My cousin Trap never changes!

But this time he was truly a **HERO**. It was thanks to him that we had managed to defeat the Great Blob!

So we organized a big party for the whole crew.

Grandfather William made an official speech. "Thank you, Benjamin and Bugsy Wugsy. You behaved like true **space** heroes. You both deserve MEDALS! And you, Sally: the idea to use superglue was brilliant!"

Then he turned to Thea. "My dear Thea, your courage and intelligence *saved* the *MouseStar 1*," he said.

Grandfather William

He walked over to Trap. "Well done, Grandson," he said, patting him on the back. "Your candy trick was very impressive. You remind me of myself when I was young!"

He even had a compliment for PROFESSOR GREENFUR. "A scientist is indispensable on a spaceship, and your expertise is valued highly!" he told the professor.

Finally, he turned to me. "Grandson, I didn't think you **had it in you**!" he said. "You really came through this time."

We TOASTED one another with Cook Squizzy's famouse cheddar shakes with chocolate space sprinkles as we recited the Creed of the Spacemice.

I, of course, couldn't wait to return to my cabin so that I could finally start *writing* my very first book. I decided to write all about this **adventure**! I hope you enjoyed reading it. Until next time, my dear mouse friends, I am Geronimo Stiltonix . . . captain of the *MOUSESTAR 1*!

THE CREED
OF THE SPACEMICE

We are the spacemice,
gentle and sure.
Our missions are good,
and our hearts are pure.

Intergalactic adventure
is the name of our game.
We'll come to the rescue,
and it's not for the fame.

Our spaceship flies
through the universe with ease.
Friendship, to us,
is more precious than cheese.

The Cheddar Galaxy
is our cosmic home.
With spacemice for friends,
you're never alone.

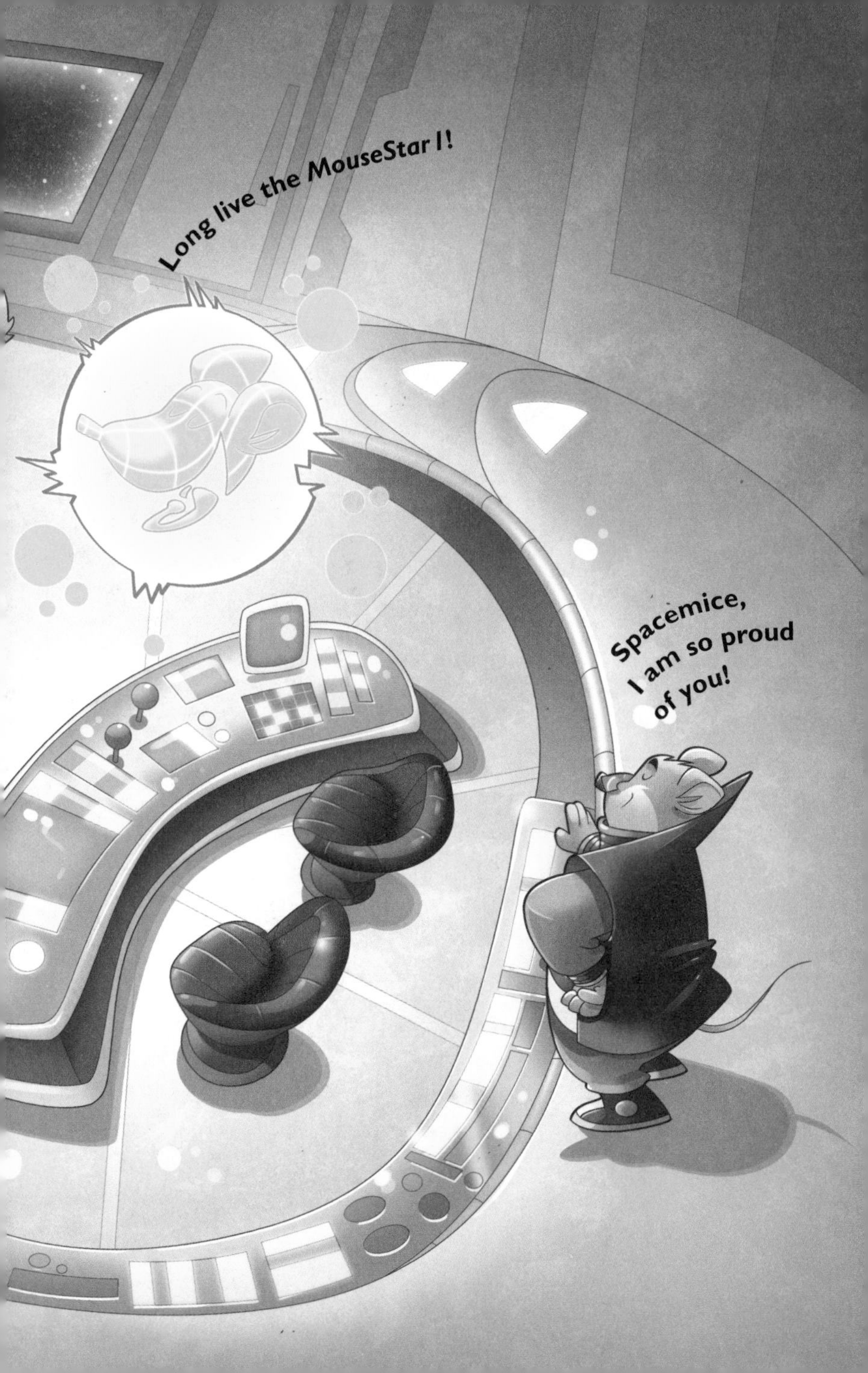
Long live the MouseStar I!
Spacemice, I am so proud of you!

Want to read the next adventure of the spacemice? I can't wait to tell you all about it!

YOU'RE MINE, CAPTAIN!

The *MouseStar 1* is contacted by strange aliens whose ship has broken down! Geronimo Stiltonix is happy to help them out, and even accompanies them to their home planet, Flurkon. But during his visit, the alien queen becomes enchanted by Geronimo — and wants to marry him! Will he be forced to stay on Flurkon forever?

Be sure to read all my fabumouse adventures!

#1 Lost Treasure of the Emerald Eye

#2 The Curse of the Cheese Pyramid

#3 Cat and Mouse in a Haunted House

#4 I'm Too Fond of My Fur!

#5 Four Mice Deep in the Jungle

#6 Paws Off, Cheddarface!

#7 Red Pizzas for a Blue Count

#8 Attack of the Bandit Cats

#9 A Fabumouse Vacation for Geronimo

#10 All Because of a Cup of Coffee

#11 It's Halloween, You 'Fraidy Mouse!

#12 Merry Christmas, Geronimo!

#13 The Phantom of the Subway

#14 The Temple of the Ruby of Fire

#15 The Mona Mousa Code

#16 A Cheese-Colored Camper

#17 Watch Your Whiskers, Stilton!

#18 Shipwreck on the Pirate Islands

#19 My Name Is Stilton, Geronimo Stilton

#20 Surf's Up, Geronimo!

#21 The Wild, Wild West

#22 The Secret of Cacklefur Castle

A Christmas Tale

#23 Valentine's Day Disaster

#24 Field Trip to Niagara Falls

#25 The Search for Sunken Treasure

#26 The Mummy with No Name

#27 The Christmas Toy Factory

#28 Wedding Crasher

#29 Down and Out Down Under

#30 The Mouse Island Marathon

#31 The Mysterious Cheese Thief

Christmas Catastrophe

#32 Valley of the Giant Skeletons

#33 Geronimo and the Gold Medal Mystery

#34 Geronimo Stilton, Secret Agent

#35 A Very Merry Christmas

#36 Geronimo's Valentine

#37 The Race Across America

#38 A Fabumouse School Adventure

#39 Singing Sensation

#40 The Karate Mouse

#41 Mighty Mount Kilimanjaro

#42 The Peculiar Pumpkin Thief

#43 I'm Not a Supermouse!

#44 The Giant
Diamond Robbery

#45 Save the White
Whale!

#46 The Haunted
Castle

#47 Run for the Hills,
Geronimo!

#48 The Mystery in
Venice

#49 The Way of
the Samurai

#50 This Hotel Is
Haunted

#51 The Enormouse
Pearl Heist

#52 Mouse in Space!

#53 Rumble in
the Jungle

#54 Get into Gear,
Stilton!

#55 The Golden
Statue Plot

#56 Flight of the
Red Bandit

Special Edition!

The Hunt for the
Golden Book

#57 The Stinky
Cheese Vacation

#58 The Super
Chef Contest

*Don't miss my journey
through time!*

Meet
GERONIMO STILTONOOT

He is a cavemouse — Geronimo Stilton's ancient ancestor! He runs the stone newspaper in the prehistoric village of Old Mouse City. From dealing with dinosaurs to dodging meteorites, his life in the Stone Age is full of adventure!

#1 The Stone of Fire

#2 Watch Your Tail!

#3 Help, I'm in Hot Lava!

#4 The Fast and the Frozen

#5 The Great Mouse Race

#6 Don't Wake the Dinosaur!

Don't miss these exciting Thea Sisters adventures!

Thea Stilton and the Dragon's Code

Thea Stilton and the Mountain of Fire

Thea Stilton and the Ghost of the Shipwreck

Thea Stilton and the Secret City

Thea Stilton and the Mystery in Paris

Thea Stilton and the Cherry Blossom Adventure

Thea Stilton and the Star Castaways

Thea Stilton: Big Trouble in the Big Apple

Thea Stilton and the Ice Treasure

Thea Stilton and the Secret of the Old Castle

Thea Stilton and the Blue Scarab Hunt

Thea Stilton and the Prince's Emerald

Thea Stilton and the Mystery on the Orient Express

Thea Stilton and the Dancing Shadows

Thea Stilton and the Legend of the Fire Flowers

Thea Stilton and the Spanish Dance Mission

Thea Stilton and the Journey to the Lion's Den

Thea Stilton and the Great Tulip Heist

Thea Stilton and the Chocolate Sabotage

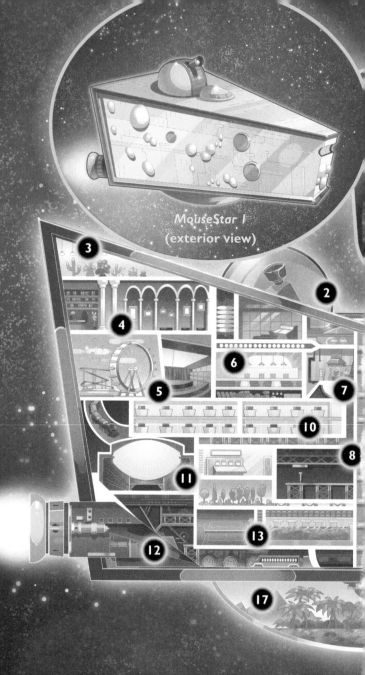

MouseStar 1

The spaceship, home, and refuge of the spacemice!

MouseStar 1
(exterior view)

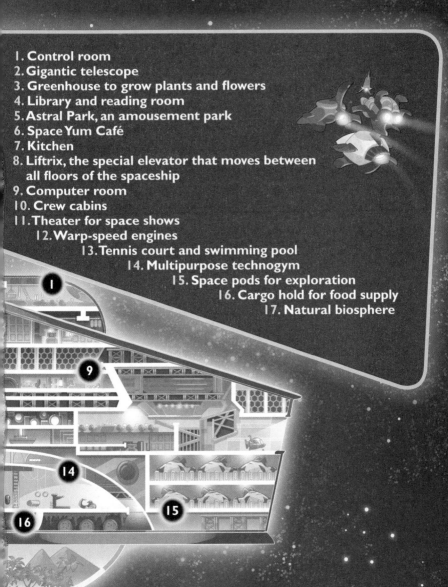

Dear mouse friends,
thanks for reading,
and good-bye until the next book.
See you in outer space!